TOM RICHTER

Basic Training

This book was professionally typeset on Reedsy.
Find out more at reedsy.com

Contents

The Himmelfeuer Saga Timeline

- <u>Summer 1943</u> – *Paragon #1: The Sexy Origins of America's Golden Sun*
- <u>February 1944</u> – *Thor #1: The Seduction of the God of Thunder*
- <u>June 6th 1944</u> – *Paragon #2: D–Day Delight*
- <u>January 23rd 1945</u> – *Thor #2 – Battle of the Bulge*
- <u>January 23rd 1945</u> – *Paragon #3 – Body Heat*
- <u>April 28th 1945</u> – *Thor #3 – Crowned With Horns*
- <u>May 2nd 1945</u> – **Berlin falls to Allied Forces.**
- <u>May 8th 1945</u> – **World War II ends in Europe with an Allied Forces Victory.**
- <u>Spring 2002</u> – *Basic Training*
- <u>Summer 2002</u> – *Advanced Training*
- <u>Spring 2008</u> – *Ranger Training*
- <u>Summer 2009</u> – *Widowmaker #1 – Tactical Sexpionage Action*
- <u>Fall 2011</u> – *Widowmaker #2 – For Your Thighs Only*
- <u>Fall 2012</u> – *Maxxx & Saphron #1*
- <u>Spring 2013</u> – *Maxxx & Saphron #2: Maxxx & Saphron Do Detroit*
- <u>Summer 2014</u> – *Widowmaker #3: Rogue Relations*
- <u>February 2015</u> – *Maxxx & Saphron #3: Operation Dongle Drop*
- <u>Spring 2015</u> – *Earth's Sexiest Heroes #1*
- <u>Summer 2016</u> – *Earth's Sexiest Heroes #2: Ragnarok Comes!*
- <u>Winter 2017</u> – *Earth's Sexiest Heroes #3: Crisis of Faith*

The Dirty DC 2016 Election Cycle Timeline

- <u>1990's thru 2010</u> — *45 Screws*
- <u>Fall 2015</u> — *The Zodiac*

1

Chapter 1

2002 C.E.

It wasn't until we stepped into the reception center of the airport that we got our first taste of what we had truly gotten ourselves into. We were greeted by a female drill sergeant complete with the trademark hat bent up on the left side, that is if you can call yelling and herding us into groups of fifty a greeting. As we sat there, a nameless throng, awaiting our turn to board the bus some chattered idly while others sat in silence their voices crushed by the weight of their decision. I closed my eyes and took a nap expecting full well to be sitting waiting for some time before the bus came and it was already well after midnight. Surprisingly enough sleep came easy and I got a nice nap before being jostled from my dreams and lined up for boarding.

The bus ride was more lighthearted. The bus driver was a jovial older fellow who delighted in telling bad jokes the likes of which you couldn't help but laugh at for their sheer absurdity. I had the pleasure of being seated next to a girl from Minnesota who wouldn't stop talking. I smiled and nodded politely as she prattled on and on about her boyfriend back home whom she loved dearly, for she reminded me of it frequently in her musings. I'm not so sure I believe it myself since she handed me a piece of paper with her name and e-mail address as the bus was pulling out to the gate of the military installation.

The bus came to a halt at the gate and we were boarded by security personnel, complete with M-4 carbines slung over their shoulders. I was itching to get my hands on one of those myself and eyed it longingly as the Corporal walked down the isle checking our ID. The others had at the moment realized just how serious things now were and sat in patient nervous silence. Before long he had made his way back to the front of the bus, where he turned and with an unexpected smile, he wished us luck and made his departure.

Alicia, her name I had gleaned from the paper she slipped me before I tucked it into my bag, turned to me nervously as we pulled away from the gate and resumed her chattering. "Oh my god, I don't know if I am ready for this. What was I thinking? I don't think I'm going to make it through this. This is the dumbest thing I've ever done. What am I going to do?"

I placed my hand gently on her knee, which she covered with her own. "You're going to do the same thing the rest of us are going to do. Rise to the occasion and shine." Did I mean it? Sure, I was ready. I was here to have fun. I was born and raised for this.

"Do you mean it? You think I can do this?" She continued to go on and on, but I stopped listening. I went back to my politely nodding here and there, removing my hand from hers and adjusting the chain around my neck.

We were being ushered off the bus before we knew it. Rushing in the direction of a Drill Sergeant who screamed all manner of obscenities mixed in with the instruction for the formation of two lines males to the right and females to the left. I stood stock still behind a tall lanky guy with long shaggy hair, bag in hand as the DS paced up and down the line pausing only to scream corrective verbal abuse in the faces of quivering nervous recruits. Before long we were trudging half asleep in two columns, males on the left and females on the right, towards our new home.

The males were sent to one end of the building the females to the other. Males were then split between two large open barracks walls lined with lockers and two long lines of beds some single, some bunks. We passed single file up one wall and back down the next stopping in front of a lock and dropping our bags. Standing in front of our lockers we waited as two grinning privates swaggered into the barracks followed by our Drill Sergeant.

"All right soldiers, welcome to the first platoon. These two will be your fire guard for the first shift. They and the others who come to relieve them will be training you throughout the rest of the night. Do as they say. If I get a bad report in the morning you can rest assured it will hurt you more than it hurts me. Hagan, get these boys into the showers." He grabbed his hat and disappeared out the door.

"Everyone loses the clothes, grab a towel on the way to the latrine, and get in the shower you have ten minutes." He sneered. "What are you waiting for? Move!" He screamed.

I've never seen people tear their clothes off so fast. I could have done without so much wang but it's unavoidable when you have fifty naked men rushing to cram into a small room with only eight shower heads and get out in ten minutes. By my watch, it was thirty minutes before the last of us staggered out and pulled our clothes back on. We stood by our beds as Hagans partner walked back to the latrine, which was in the rear of the barracks, and peered in through the door.

"Why the hell is this floor wet? Get your asses back here and dry this floor!" He yelled as the ten nearest to him scrambled towels in hand past him. They scrambled around on their hands and knees sopping up water as others went in to help them. Before long they were all being rushed back out to stand in front of their lockers.

Hagan stood before a bed that lay in the center of the room looking around at everyone. "One last thing before you hit the rack. You have to be initiated to the company."

"Everyone loose your pants and gather round." Hagan's cronies announced.

We did as we were instructed and gathered around the bed. It wasn't till I was next to it that I realized there was a human form underneath the blankets. Hagan reached to draw the blankets off as I braced myself for some horrible joke. As the blankets drew back I, like everyone else, stared blankly at the beautiful young woman lying before us sky-clad. I was lost as to the meaning, if it was a joke I wasn't getting the punchline. I was however growing firm in my desire to have this woman, whoever she may be.

"Everyone here is no doubt familiar with a circle jerk, well get to it. We've provided wank material and we want her covered from head to toe, at which time you will be full-fledged members of Bravo Company." Hagan stated in his usual commanding tone. "Well, boys get to it! Don't be shy."

I didn't have to be told twice. I grasped by already erect member in my left hand and began pumping, slowly at first, tuning out the grunts of the others around me. The sight of loads jettisoned by the others only spurned me on, stroking faster and faster feeling my charge building and priming to burst. After each man left his mark, they stepped back limp and exhausted, to make room for someone else. I quivered and shot a hot steamy load across her face, the first drops of which caused her to open her mouth to catch the rest and lick her lips. I was about to step back when I realized I wasn't going flaccid as one usually does.

I continued not once but twice more. When I finished I was the only one standing over her. Hagan slapped me on the back and smiled. "She must have done something real special for you there chief. I've never seen anything like that before." I looked down into her now-open eyes sparkling in the dim lights of the barracks. I was breathlessly drawn into the deep cool gray pools, lost for a moment until her smile jerked me from the reverie.

She stood up and walked off towards the latrine, stopping briefly only to glance at me over her shoulder before disappearing into the showers. I returned to my bed, pulled on my clothes, and tried to banish her from my thoughts. No one had ever had such an effect on me, captured me so completely.

Hagan's cronies stood at the foot of my bed surveying the room. "Everyone hit the rack!" He yelled. "You," he jabbed a finger in my direction. "to the latrine. You've got a mess to clean up."

I expected this to be some manner of further hazing, last man done sort of thing. I shuffled my way down the length of the barracks and into the latrine. All the showers were running hot the steam filled the changing room obscuring everything. I decided it best to strip off my clothes, tossing them on the bench that ran along the walls of the room and made my way into the showers.

She was standing there, light-colored brown hair clinging to her body, when she saw me she smiled. Already I felt the blood engorging my unit at the mere sight of her. I drew closer to her, uncertain what I was supposed to do, and fighting the urge to take her. She grasped my hands as soon as I came within reach and pulled me to her, pressing her glistening flesh against mine. "They said I had a mess to clean up, but I'm not sure what I'm supposed to be doing in here." The words had barely escaped my lips before she placed a finger over them silencing me.

She took my penis into her hands and playfully tugged at it and caressed it. She nibbled at my ear and then whispered, "You are to be the platoon sergeant, with all the responsibilities," her whispers trailed off as she licked my lips and kissed me lightly before moving to the other ear and continuing. "And all the benefits thereof."

I was speechless. Once again I fell into her eyes as she artfully sent shudders through my entire being with but the slightest flitting of fingers along the shaft and head in her hands. She planted another kiss on my lips, then sank ever so slowly to her knees covering my chest and stomach with kisses along the way. Before I realized what had happened I was in her mouth, her tongue skillfully darting to and fro to make my arms flail about looking for something to grasp onto lest I lose my balance in the waves of ecstasy. She played at this, it seemed, forever before I felt the shuddering of my shaft in her mouth, squeezing a warm gout down her throat which she gulped down then licked the head repeatedly to make sure she didn't miss a drop. It was too much to handle, my legs buckled under me, and had I not been holding on to the towel bars attached to the walls, I would have crashed to the floor.

I regained my footing and came to realize that I remained firm in her hands as she returned to her feet. "My aren't you the specimen," she whispered, looking down at my still-hard cock in her adept hands. She ran a finger up and down my chest then stepped away to the wall opposite us, where she grasped two towel bars bending over slightly at the waist. She shot a look back at me that told me clearly what was to be done next.

As if in a dream I glided across the gulf between us and was in her. The warmth that ran through me was euphoric as I slid slowly deeper and she too shuddered with it and let out a quiet moan. I went slowly at first, slipping millimeter by millimeter between her dripping lips. "Faster faster." she cried out, her voice revealing the maddening effect I had produced with my torturous slowness.

I drew out a few more strokes before obliging her demands. With the quickening of pace which followed so too grew the volume and frequency of the moans uttered from her gasping mouth. I imagined for a moment how hard it must be for those just beyond these walls to sleep with her screams echoing off the latrine walls, but then I drove on faster feeling the tightening around me of her cumming. This only made her louder crying out, "Cum inside me." over and over again.

It was then that I realized, or more accurately hoped, that she had made some use of contraceptive as I certainly hadn't even thought of it in the heat of things.

The thought passed quickly, as it was too late to do anything about it anyway. I continued pounding away at her, my legs once again beginning to fail me. I could feel it coming to the surface, ready to blow at any moment like an erupting volcano. With one final violent thrust, I came inside her, her cunt still contracting around me. She let out one last scream of delight as I fell to the ground my legs no longer able to sustain my weight.

She slid her fingers between her legs retrieving some of my fluid before sucking it off her fingers. She knelt next to my exhausted body and whispered, "Never have I tasted a man so good."

I don't know what happened after that. I only dimly remember her leaving me there the showers pouring water down on me. I awoke hours, clothed, in my bed, to the tune of reveille. The OJT, on-the-job training, fire guards yelled and screamed that we were to remain in bed until told otherwise. I, feeling exhausted and wondering if it had all been some sort of dream, was not about to argue with more sleep. Just as I was drifting off I heard the voice of one of the OJT-ers saying. "I heard you made Platoon Sergeant. Congratulations you lucky bastard." Then I drifted off into peaceful slumber.

2

Chapter 2

We were woken sometime later by two screaming drill sergeants who rushed us through morning hygiene practices and downstairs into formation. We were instructed to form four ranks of equal length. There were four lines painted on the ground which were intended to be used as a guide. To my surprise, this exercise went rather well and we were then led off to lunch, as we had been allowed to sleep through breakfast.

We were forming up after lunch, under the scrutinizing eye of our head drill sergeant, Sgt. Smith, when we were called to attention suddenly and Sgt. Smith rendered a salute to someone I couldn't see because a support pillar blocked my line of sight. I heard a female voice say, "Carry on" and we were put at ease. It was then that she passed into view. The woman I had thought for sure was a dream. She made brief eye contact with me and then continued on her path. That was when I noticed the silver bar of her first lieutenant rank on her shoulder.

"That, soldiers, is our XO lieutenant Gates. She'll be around from time to time, checking in on training when we go out to the ranges over the next ten weeks."

We spent the rest of the day going over basic drill movements and I was given a brief overview as to my responsibilities as platoon sergeant, which was not an actual rank increase just a position here in training. I had difficulty concentrating and found myself caught up in daydreams about Lt. Gates several times. I managed to avoid looking too stupid though and was never responsible for corrective physical exertion as Sgt. Smith liked to call us doing a great deal many push-ups. By the time we were released for showers and lights out our arms could barely sustain our weight any longer and we were all glad to finally be able to get some sleep.

The rest of the week was devoted to the process of in-processing. Uniform issues, shots, physical examination, blood testing, urinalyses, all that fun stuff. In between appointments, we had classes covering rank recognition and suicide. We were also given the soldier's bible. A handbook that contained everything we were going to need to know by the end of the ten weeks. We were expected to spend every free moment with our noses firmly entrenched in the book reading and committing to memory the entire book.

Saturday was relatively laid back. We were expected only to clean up the barracks and then were left more or less alone. The Drill Sergeant on duty, Sgt Greenway, checked in every so often just to make sure we weren't sleeping or sitting on our beds. I took the time to wander around the room and get to know the platoon a little better. I was expected to find four squad leaders before Monday and after watching all week long I narrowed it down and informed them. To my surprise, none of them turned it down and I set them to finding team leaders for their respective squads.

After dinner, we were sent up to our barracks to await further instruction. After about ten minutes Drill Sergeant Greenway entered and called everyone to gather around the desk at the front of the room.

"Saturday nights we usually do something special around here. As you know the barracks upstairs houses the females of the third platoon. Well, I was just up there running this by them and they had no complaints. So from now on, unless you piss me off, you will be spending Saturday nights up there with them." He said quite plainly.

"Excuse me Drill Sergeant but what exactly do you mean by "Up there with them?"" Someone asked.

"I mean Saturday night orgy. Now I know most of you have never been with a woman before and wouldn't even know where to begin. But I'm sure Johnson here can give you a few pointers." He looked at me and smirked. "Isn't that right Johnson?"

"Yes Drill Sergeant," I replied.

"Well, what are you waiting for an engraved invitation? Get up there and get your freak on." That was all it took. Everyone was on their feet and bolting out the door, Sgt. Greenway grabbed me by the shoulder and pulled me aside as everyone rushed past. "You come with me. Lt. Gates wants to see you personally. When she's done with you you can join the rest of the platoon.

I made my way downstairs, Sgt. Greenway heading upstairs to oversee the orgy taking place without me. Judging by the noise I gathered second and fourth platoons were also engaging in acts of reckless abandon. I entered the Command Quarters and made my way to the XO's office. I stood at attention at the door and knocked once. "Enter." I was told and I positioned myself in front of her desk making all appropriate facing movements along the way.

"Ma'am, Private Johnson reports as ordered." I was glad I had remembered proper procedure and not just walked in like a fool. I had no intention of looking a fool in front of this amazing woman.

"Stand at ease, Johnson. Do you know why I brought you down here?"

"No ma'am."

She stood and walked around in front of me. I caught the faint scent of lilac as she came closer. "Johnson, I like to keep in touch with my platoon sergeants." She sat on her desk legs spread revealing her cleanly shaven nether region in the shadow of her skirt. "I like to know what's going on with my troops straight from their leadership. That way I know the drill sergeants aren't keeping anything from me. So tell me, Johnson, are my troops happy?"

"Yes ma'am. There have been few complaints, mostly about having to get used to waking so early, but otherwise we have a good strong group I think. I've selected four squad leaders that I've noticed take charge and offer assistance to those around them. I'd say if nothing else they are eager to get to training now that all this processing is done with."

"What about you Johnson, how are you taking your leadership role?" She asked as she ran a pen along her lips and placed it in her mouth, distracting me for a moment before I answered.

"So far so good. Everyone seems responsive to me. I've had no arguments against my methods for daily duty rotations."

"Good to hear. Good to hear." She began unbuttoning her blouse slowly starting from the bottom revealing the alabaster skin concealed beneath. "Well then Johnson, you are free to go join your platoon. Unless of course, you'd prefer to stay here with me."

No man in his right mind would refuse this woman. Her right hand made its way up her skirt fingers parting the lips and sliding out of sight while the left kneaded one breast and then the other. I stood there, staring, uncertain how to proceed. I don't know how long I stood there before her hand shot out and grabbed my shirt pulling me a hair's breadth from her lips.

"What's wrong Johnson, don't you want to play?" Before I could answer her tongue was in my mouth flicking around sporadically and I could feel the buttons on my shirt being yanked loose. My hands groped for her firm breasts squeezing them and grazing the rock-hard nipples stopping only long enough for my shirt and undershirt to be pulled off. I unlaced my boots with some difficulty and tore them off tossing them aside, my pants quick to follow as I ripped off her skirt and buried my face between her legs.

I parted the mound with my fingers and ran my tongue around her clit in slow deliberate circles. She dug her fingers into my back as I started lapping faster, sliding two fingers inside her sacred well. Her nails bit deeper as my pace increased driven on and on by the moans escaping from deep within her. My jaw was beginning to grow numb when her screams crescendoed and I felt the contracting muscles of orgasm tightening around my fingers.

I was pulled to my feet and we toppled backwards onto the desk our lips joined passionately and tongues darting about playfully. Without a thought I was in her, feeling the final quaking and contractions as I slowly delved into the depths. I maintained my slow torturous pace regardless of her screams and demands for more. Then when it seemed she was on the verge of tears I began pounding away at her with all the force and speed I could muster.

Next thing I knew I was seated on the desk, fully in her mouth. She looked up at me and I was lost in her eyes. I could hear only the gasps and moans I uttered reverberating in my dreamscape. The pressure building within me pulled me deeper into her eyes. I flailed around for something to grab before getting entangled firmly in her hair. Just before I burst she pulled her head back smiling at the cum splashing across her face. She licked her lips and wiped off her face with her skirt. We collapsed together on the floor enfolded in each other's arms. We drifted off to sleep wrapped in a blanket pulled out of a nearby cabinet.

That night I dreamed of home. For three years before coming here, I had been with a girl who I thought loved me, who I thought I loved. We hadn't talked of the future but in my mind, it was me and her forever. She was in my dreams, she had been frequently in the weeks that had passed since she left me. Enlistment was my dream, always had been, she never liked it and when the time came she wouldn't have it. It was her likeness that haunted my sleep leaving me disoriented in waking.

"Johnson."

"Yes ma'am?"

"Gather your uniform and remove yourself from my office." Lt. Gates ordered, buttoning the last button on her blouse and seating herself behind the desk.

"Proceeding ma'am." Quickly I dressed and disappeared from the room. Making my way upstairs, thoughts of the Lieutenant freed my mind of the depression dreams had left upon me. She was one hell of a woman, that was for sure.

3

Chapter 3

I arrived in the barracks just in time for reveille. Everyone went about the morning rituals of dressing, bed making, and personal hygiene Dressed already, and bed untouched from the night before, I grabbed my toothbrush, toothpaste, and electric razor from my locker and retired to the latrine. I was in the middle of brushing my teeth when Sammy Garcia, a short Mexican guy who slept two bunks over, took the sink next to me and started shaving.

"Where were you last night Johnson? You missed all the fun." Garcia asked over the buzzing of several razors.

"Lt. Gates called me to her office. Wanted to take a meeting with me about the moral of the platoon." I answered after spitting out a mouth full of suds.

"You stuck it to her no?" his smirk was accompanied by a raised eyebrow.

"Garcia, is that all you think about?" I added one more razor hum to the droning that echoed around us.

"You know it sarge. Last night the ladies weren't complaining though. I may not be packing, but let me tell you when I get going I'm like a jackhammer. I get those ladies quaking over and over again before I bust my nut. The chicas upstairs can confirm that for you."

"Garcia Garcia Garcia, do you kiss your mother with that mouth?"

"Johnson, you should be more concerned with what this mouth did to your mother."

"Have you seen pictures of my mother?" I finished shaving and gathered my belongings.

"No, why how much do you want for the pictures?" He began brushing his teeth confident he had gotten the last word.

"You couldn't afford my mother's picture, much less my mother. Not on E-1 salary." I walked out before he could reply, not wishing for the smack talk to go on all day.

With the morning tasks completed, we made our retreat downstairs for formation. We were greeted by Drill Sergeant Gunn, who was easily the most hardcore of the company's drill sergeants. Some would say he took his job too seriously, others that he enjoyed it. I thought he just wanted to leave his mark by graduating nothing less than the best-trained soldiers around. We were to be his last group which was just one more reason to push us harder than all the rest.

The platoon sergeants were ordered to march their platoons to chow. After chow, we were to form up and await further instruction. I led the march with my platoon up front it was our turn to eat first. After packing down as much food as I could load onto my tray, I joined my formation and quizzed them on various subjects from the soldier's bible. It wasn't long before the other platoons were fed and formed up and Sgt. Gunn came out of the CQ.

"As you all know today is Sunday." He began. "Many if not all of you, are no doubt wondering about chapel services. Over there," He pointed to a small table that normally sat inside CQ, "is a sheet with all the various chapel services listed with times and which stop you need to get off the bus. The bus stop is on the other side of the battalion and comes by every fifteen minutes, I suggest you get out there a bit early. Sign out on the book that sits on the table when you leave, and sign back in when you get back. You will go to and only to your chapel service. You won't make any trips to the BX, McDonald's, or any other place your dumbasses might think it'd be fun to sneak off to. If you go out there acting like a bunch of jackasses and make me look bad I will personally expedite your ass off this base and out of my military." There was a pause to let the weight of it settle in before he continued. "If you're not at church, then the rest of the day is yours to do laundry, get your lockers up to snuff, write letters, or whatever it is you knuckleheads do up there when I'm not around. I will be coming and going from time to time to check in on you so don't let me catch you up there sleeping or sitting on the bunks." He turned to talk away, then faced us once more. "If you get the bright idea to act a fool with members of the opposite gender, don't even think about it. I know all about last night's festivities and it will be limited to Saturday nights only. Don't let me catch anybody in a barracks of the opposite gender. You're all dismissed, you will be called down to form up when it is time for lunch." He left us there and the platoon sergeants took charge calling their respective charges to attention and then giving them the order to fall out.

More or less everyone headed to the table to find out when their church service was. I having noticed the same bulletin upstairs in the barracks just walked calmly up the stairs and checked the times there. Noting that I had two hours before the Baptist service, I went to work making sure my locker was up to standards. My locker was a mess since I had spent yesterday getting to know everyone under my charge while they were taking the time to get their lockers in order. It took most of the two hours to get everything in order, leaving just enough time to write a short letter home before signing out and heading to the bus stop with all the other Baptists in the company.

The service was uplifting, though far too much of it was devoted to explaining how the bible related to some of the more tedious and annoying tasks we had to complete such as folding our Government Issue BVD's in a certain way to pass inspections. I was very interested in their explanation of why it was okay for us to kill people because "God always forgives a soldier.". I was, however, a little annoyed by the references to us being God's soldiers. While I was a Christian and had been for as long as I can remember, I was never the kind of Christian who was so blindly devoted that I condemned all other religions as barbarian heathens who didn't know any better. Especially since one good look at the Muslim and Jewish beliefs shows that their holy books and the bible were derived from the same source. That we kill and conquer in the name of God and the U.S.A. just seemed like blasphemy and arrogance to me. Regardless of it all though, I came out of the service feeling spiritually recharged. I was on my way to bible study when an arm reached out from the female latrine and pulled me in while no one was looking.

I was dragged to the last stall in the row and pressed against the tiled wall before I had any clue what was going on. Pushed tightly against me was Alicia the girl I had sat next to on the bus the night we had arrived. Her face was only inches from mine and a smile beamed across her face. Her shining eyes looked up into mine, she was at least a good foot shorter than me, and her hands lay upon my heaving chest.

"I'm so glad you came to this service." She said in a whisper. "Ever since we sat together on the bus I haven't been able to stop thinking about you."

I stood there, unsure what to do, slightly aroused by the pressure from her body and the sweet smell in her hair. Without thinking I placed my hands on her waist and drew her tighter against me.

"I was hoping to catch your attention last night, but you didn't show. You're the Platoon Sergeant, ours got called away too. She said she spent the night with the first sergeant. I assume you had a similar encounter." She lowered her eyes as though she couldn't bear to look at me while awaiting my answer.

"I did." I could see that the answer pained her.

"Last night when you weren't there... I locked myself in a stall in the latrine and cried. I cried till long after everyone else had exhausted themselves and gone to sleep. I didn't want to be with anyone else, I just wanted to be with you." She looked back up at me the tears welling up in her eyes, waiting to break and surge down her face.

I smiled down at her. I had no idea what to do. She had feelings for me, for someone she knew nothing about and had watched from afar over the last week. What could I do, what could I say?

I didn't get a chance to say anything before she kissed me. Her soft lips sent a spark through me as they connected to mine. I wrapped my arms around her and poured every ounce of passion in me into kissing her back. A few minutes passed that seemed like an eternity then she began hastily groping at my clothes pulling them off, enticing me to respond in kind. Her body was tanned from head to toe and pristine clean shaven not a hair on any part of her save her head. I could smell the sweet juices flowing between her legs before I dipped my fingers into her sacred spring and began toying with her miniature organ. She moaned softly in my ear then bit into my neck to stifle further moaning and gasping, lest anyone should hear. Moments later she was biting deep into my shoulder and quivering wildly before she fell back onto the toilet seat panting heavily a few drops of blood on her lips.

She grasped the erect member before her and began pumping away while catching her breath. The moment her breathing returned to normal she took me into her mouth, gazing up at me with her gorgeous green eyes full of affection. She licked and sucked in ways that showed she was no stranger to this sort of thing, it didn't take her long to draw the fluids from me, though she struggled and choked a little in swallowing the viscous liquid. I smiled at this, for someone who disliked it to make the effort gave me a warm fuzzy feeling. She continued to lick every last drop free of me noticing as I did that I remained full and hard in her hands.

I grabbed her by her hair, which made her gasp and shudder, and turned her away from me bent over at the waist. She held herself up by holding on to the toilet pipes in front of her. I slid slowly into her then about halfway in I made a quick violent thrust that caught her off guard and nearly slammed her head into the fixtures as a result. She braced herself more firmly for this sort of treatment and began railing away at her with quick hard thrusts followed by slow torturous withdrawals. I reveled in her moans and squeals of delight, watching her breasts bounce back and forth as I pounded her harder and harder. Her moans turned into screams and I felt the contractions of orgasm upon me again and again before I could no longer contain myself, deploying my doomed legions deep inside her.

I withdrew and she sank upon the toilet once more letting the fluids drip from her while she struggled to catch her breath once again. I kissed her on the cheek and then began dressing my own breathless body.

Once I was dressed I glanced at my watch. Bible study would be over in a few minutes. We didn't have long before we would have to make our way back to the battalion and rejoin our respective platoons. I helped her with her clothes, then we made a discreet and luckily unnoticed exit from the latrine. Bible study ended shortly thereafter and we joined the throng as it made its chattering buzzing way to the bus stop and onboard the waiting vehicle. Once we were seated on the bus, next to each other once again, she grabbed my hand and took it in hers concealed only barely by the bible bag she carried with her. I didn't fight it, though I was leery that someone would notice it brought that warm fuzzy feeling to me again. I wasn't sure, but I suspected I was beginning to fall for her. I stole a glance over at her and noticed she was staring intently out the window, but I did catch a glimmer of a smile embedded on her smooth almost angelic face.

Once back in the barracks, the full weight of things came down upon me. I was conflicted now between the breathtaking beauty of Lt. Gates and the passionate affections of Alicia. Luckily I was distracted from my brooding by the call to lunch which required me to put my thoughts aside and take charge of my platoon.

Lunch left something to be desired. Not the finest meal served in the dining facility over the last week, it was a leading candidate for the worst though the looks on most everyone's faces confirmed that I was not alone in this assertion. After lunch, we returned to our quarters to continue going about our business. I gathered up my laundry and headed down to the laundry room hoping that I wasn't going to walk into a hopelessly crowded line to use the machines. Luckily there were only a few ahead of me, so I plopped down on my laundry bag and tried in vain to distract myself with the methods of operating and maintaining the M249 Squad Automatic Weapon.

Now when I can't seem to get engrossed in the specifications of a fine piece of weaponry like a S.A.W. then there is something wrong. After reading the same line four times over I closed the book and returned it to my right cargo pocket. I could do nothing but focus on the dilemma at hand. First, there was the executive officer, who had dominated my thoughts since our first encounter. She was simply amazing, too amazing actually. I began to wonder just how many platoon sergeants had come before me. I felt the stinging pain of the realization that I was just another plaything and I wouldn't be the last. Some part of me fell to pieces at the revelation that there was no future in the encounters with her beyond the next nine weeks.

Alicia on the other hand I didn't know what to think about. Since the night on the bus, I hadn't even so much as given her a second thought. Our brief meeting at the chapel on the other hand left an impression on me that I couldn't shake.

She was confusing, to say the least. On the bus, she had done nothing but talk about her boyfriend back home but she took the time to scribble out her name and means to contact her and slip it to me. From her passionate speech this morning I could conclude only two things, either she was a superb actress to display such emotion falsely, or I was dominating her thoughts as Lt. Gates was mine. What I couldn't discern was my feelings regarding her.

I was jarred from my internal debate by an opening door. "Johnson!" yelled one of my squad leaders.

"Kraft!" I answered enthusiastically.

"Johnson, I've been meaning to talk to you. Man to man." Kraft sat down next to me, folding his hat at placing it in his cargo pocket.

"Well, here I am, what's on your mind?" I had no idea where this was going. I barely knew the guy I hardly felt this warranted a male bonding moment already.

"Johnson, me and a couple of the others, hell damn near everyone else, have noticed your preoccupation with a certain executive officer. Now don't get me wrong, she's a fine piece of work and I'd love to get my hands on her just once like you have, but you're missing out on the big picture." Despite his serious tone, I was having a hard time not laughing at the words coming out of his mouth.

"Big picture?"

"Well, I'm assuming you were with Lt. Gates last night while the rest of us were in third platoon barracks. Well, while you were down there doing whatever it was you were doing, I nailed three fine young women."

"Three?"

"Three." He held up three fingers to help drive the point home.

"Only three?" I was smirking now at the absurdity of this conversation.

"Well I kept rotating between them, no one else was willing to tag out with me, otherwise it would have been more." There was an air of disappointment to his words.

"Kraft, I misjudged you, you are a man of far more principle than I had imagined."

"Johnson pay attention here. You spent a couple of hours with one woman, a knock out mind you, but she's just a plaything. Women are playthings and you have singled one out when there is a whole toy box full of them to be had. Why limit yourself like that? Those girls up there, they'll do just about anything. If you find one who won't do something you can find three or four others who will. It's paradise man, it's so beautiful it brings a tear to my eye just thinking about it."

"I'll keep all that in mind. But I'll have you know that while you were at Bible study I was in the latrine with one of them, so I'm not missing out all that much. You've only got me beat by one girl this weekend."

"You defiled a girl in the chapel? I don't know if I should be offended or proud of you. That's a holy place."

"Holy place? It was the latrine, besides I'm pagan. In my book sex is a holy act, so what better place than in a church."

"Why would a pagan go to Baptist services?"

"Pagan doesn't mean godless. Nowhere in my book does it say I can't accept Jesus and choose to know him in a different way than you do?" I was ready for a religious debate, but luckily he wasn't the type to preach to me about my wrongdoings.

"You do your thing and I'll do mine. It's not my job to save souls other than my own." He pulled out his hat and stood looking down at me. "Just remember, you may never have an opportunity like this again. Don't miss out on a beautiful thing." He held up three fingers in front of his face once more.

"Kraft you're insane," I replied no longer able to hold back a laugh.

"Just think about it Johnson, your wildest fantasies could come true."

He left me there to contemplate it once more. He spoke a certain truth about Lt. Gates. I had already concluded that my preoccupation with her was futile. He failed to realize one thing though, not everyone in the world is interested in getting as many women under his belt as possible. It had never been my style to just fool around with anyone and everyone I could get my hands on. And yet, I had done just that with not one but two women in the last twenty-four hours. Sure there were feelings attached, but they were confusing and unexplored at best. I stood and moved to a new free washing machine, this was going to take a lot of thinking out before it could be resolved.

4

Chapter 4

The next week was devoted to more classes and drill movements. Much to the approval of the Drill Sergeants, my squad leaders performed excellently, especially Kraft who seemed to have a natural talent for it. I found myself spending most of my free time conversing with Kraft, who I found I had a lot in common with despite our differing approaches to the fairer sex. The classes covered that week were Military history, which was easily my favorite class, uniform wear, first aid, and values and ethics.

Throughout the week I found myself noticing Alicia more and more. When we were standing in formations, marching to and from classes, and at meals my eyes were inexplicably drawn to her. I often looked towards her only to find that she was already watching me intently and a smile played briefly over her face before she would turn away to pay closer attention to whatever she was doing. On rare occasions, it would be her that caught me staring at her, but I looked away quickly without the flash of a smile. By the end of the week, I realized where Lt. Gates had once been embedded in the back of my mind, she had now been replaced by this mysterious little girl from Minnesota in whose mind I no doubt held a similar position.

Saturday morning came along before we knew it, much to the delight of everyone around me. I had come to dread its approach, thinking of Alicia almost exclusively now but knowing that I would be required to report to Lt. Gates to give my weekly report. I addressed my concern and confusion to

Kraft, whose only advice was to tap them both for all their worth and try to find some others to take on the side as well. "You only live once, and you're never going to have an opportunity like this again. Tap them all and let god sort it out." Was his final say on the matter, before I took my leave to check on some ruckus that was coming from the other end of our spacious abode.

Over the day I concluded that I would just have to turn the Lieutenant down and see what happened. I would have been lying if I said I didn't fear it becoming some sort of insubordination issue. All I could do was hope for the best and wait till I was expected to report and choke down the last meal of the day.

I looked over and saw her smile. Weakly I returned it, doing my damnedest not to betray any of my internal conflict.

Everyone was rushing upstairs as I pushed past them and down to ground level and into the CQ office. I walked through the small cramped office to the door which bore a placard that read Executive Officer Lt. Miranda Gates. Straightening my uniform I knocked once and stood waiting till I was beckoned to enter.

"Ma'am, Private Johnson reports as ordered." I stood stock still at attention avoiding laying my eyes upon her.

"At ease, Johnson." She shuffled some papers on her desk, placed them in a folder, and crammed them into a drawer. "What is the state of the platoon's morale, how are they reacting to training?"

"We've had some rough spots, especially with stragglers when it comes to physical fitness training, but all and all it's going just fine. Some of the more fit soldiers have taken to helping those that need and are willing to accept the help. Others have offered assistance in the academic areas for those who are struggling with committing much to memory in short periods. I expect we'll be seeing the whole platoon graduate in nine weeks, which seems like a rarity to me. I can't imagine you get a group so willing to work together very often."

"No, we don't, I can't think of a single time where we didn't lose at least one member of the platoon to failed physical training, discipline issues, or the like. If you can lead your entire platoon through to graduation I'll make sure you see a promotion before you leave this company." She smiled and stood up, moving around the desk to sit atop it in front of me, legs uncrossed and revealing her pantiless crotch glistening slightly from building moisture, in the pale light.

"Is that a challenge Ma'am?" I smirked then realized I was overstepping my bounds with such a smart assed remark and quickly wiped it off my face.

"You think you can handle it?" She let her hair cascade down from the bun that had constrained it atop her head and shook it out.

"Yes ma'am." I was beginning to get nervous, soon I would have to make my desire to join the rest of the platoon upstairs instead of staying here with her and I didn't know how to even begin approaching the subject.

"Well, we'll just have to see if you're up to the task. Do you have anything else to add to your report?"

That was as good an opening to broach the subject as I was going to get, so I drew in a deep breath and gathered my resolve. "Ma'am There is one last thing. The men have expressed their desire to have me join them on Saturday nights. I think they would feel more comfortable knowing I was just one of them and not letting the position I've been given go to my head."

"And you would give up my company to bond with your men?" She hopped up from her desk and walked around behind me opening what sounded like her cabinet and rifling through its contents.

"In the interest of morale, yes Ma'am I would." I was beginning to wonder if my ruse was working or if she suspected it was merely a veil to conceal my desires.

"Well, Johnson, if that's how you feel then you are free to join them." The door slammed behind me and in a serious breech of baring, I swung around in shock in time to see her lock the door. "But make no mistake, I will have you before you do."

I was shoved backward onto her desk before I could recover from the unexpected change in the situation. She lept atop me, as I struggled beneath her. My wrists were seized and quickly bound to the desk. My pants were torn free in clumsy haste and I was inside her. My struggling turned instead to squirming and moaning as she rocked her hips slowly against mine. She rode me hard against the desk until she had her fill and I lay sore and exhausted.

Once she finished straightening herself in the mirror she tossed me my pants. "You are dismissed, Johnson." She pushed me out the door half naked clutching the rest of my uniform.

I cleaned myself up in the CQ latrine and made my way outside. I could hear the orgy of moans and wails the moment I stepped into the night air, but it did little to prepare me for the wall-to-wall tangle of limbs of over two hundred people engaged in wanton, passionate sex.

The first thing that sticks out is Garcia's hairy ass pounding away at some blonde. Like a jackhammer, the little guy wasn't exaggerating.

I waded through the mass of limbs. Moans, and groans, past Kraft who held up four fingers and grinned at me from behind a red hand holding on for dear life to the underside of the top bunk while he put it to her with a fury. Alicia had hidden in the latrine the week before, it stood to reason she would do so again. What I found was not what I expected.

I pushed open the door and found all the stalls empty. In the small dressing room attached to the showers, I found her getting plugged by three of my men. Tears streamed from her eyes and she gazed at me with an utterly devoid of the adoration that gleamed there hours before. Filled with a combination of anger and despair I staggered out of the latrine and stumbled onto the nearest bunk. I could not feel anything, not even the pleasure of the woman who had her way with me while I stared blankly up at the ceiling. If my hands caressed her skin it was of their own accord and my mind registered nothing. I don't remember falling asleep or even going back downstairs.

5

Chapter 5

When morning came the emptiness was waiting for me. The painful image hounded me through breakfast, which I dared not look away from until I was finally able to distract myself with locker maintenance. The would be no church for me that day, I wasn't in the mood for god.

Lunch came and went, and with it my ability to preoccupy myself with menial tasks. I tried writing home, but nothing seemed worth putting to paper. My friends and family could make do without talk of dominating executive officers and company orgies.

"Johnson!"

"Kraft!" I welcomed the distraction, even if the talk would inevitably turn into a detailed discussion about the previous night's sexploits.

"What's wrong sarge? You haven't made your rounds." Kraft said sitting down next to me.

Nothing, just keeping myself busy. Keeping my shit straight instead of worrying about everyone else for once."

"Bullshit." He replied. "We both know no one keeps their shit stowed as pristine as you. On your worst day, I'd be amazed to find a single thing out of place." Exaggeration, but not far off. " Let me guess, this has to do with that tight little piece of ass you've been eye-humping all week long."

"Yeah, something like that." Not the direction I was hoping things would go.

"Let me tell you about bitches. Bitches ain't nothing but tricks and hoes."

"He ain't lying," Garcia said as he walked by.

"I tried the one woman, marriage, and monogamy road, and let me tell you there's nothing but potholes down that path. Gave me two things, a son and a glimpse at the true nature of a woman. Bitch was giving it up left and right while I worked my ass off, and for a while, we weren't even sure the boy was mine. Don't get me wrong, I love the little guy to death, but I wish to god he'd been born to a good home and not the whore he calls mommy."

"Are you going somewhere with this?" I interrupted

"Look man, I don't know what happened last night, but you're all bent out of shape over this girl you didn't even know three weeks ago. Get over it. Move on. By my count, you fucked at least two chicks last night, and while that's only half my count, by my reckoning you fucked her over just the same. I know you love this shit more than some piece of ass. Don't let last night ruin your career here."

I found his words oddly comforting. "Bitches." I replied with half a smile.

"Nothing but tricks and hoes."

The rest of the day we talked about home, his son, and inevitably his conquests. The man took great pride in two things, his son, and setting a new personal record of four chicks in one night. Hell, even I thought it was impressive. He was determined to do better by the end of the cycle.

The following week marked the end of the first phase of training, referred to as the indoctrination, or red phase. Where the last two weeks weeded out selfishness, this week pushed the limits of fear and began casting our forms into killers.

The first step of turning us into killers consisted of drilled movements for personal defense and gutting someone with an M16A2 assault rifle with a bayonet affixed beneath the barrel. Completely impractical on the modern battlefield, but a time-tested part of training nonetheless.

Drill Sergeant Greenway shared my sentiments and slammed a magazine into his rifle, pulled back the charging handle, and dropped to a prone position to aim whoever his demonstration partner happened to be when it was his turn to take us out. If you're in a position to thrust a bayonet into a man's gut, you might as well pull the trigger and save yourself some effort.

As for the rest of the week, we spent two days climbing ropes, and walls, repelling down towers, and otherwise pushing everyone's tolerance of heights. More than I expected found these tasks daunting, many more daunting than even they imagined, while others shined. The real test lies in the tasks requiring trust in each other for safe and successful navigation of an obstacle. The beginning of everyone working as a family. By the time the weekend rolled around, there wasn't a person who couldn't identify every other soldier in his platoon.

Saturday night I reported to Lt. Gates and afterward, I did my best to take Kraft's words to heart. I let myself get caught up in the throes of others' passions and desires, and were I Kraft, or any other man, I'd have felt the conqueror. Instead, I felt only emptiness.

The whole next week I couldn't sleep no matter what I tried. I picked up extra shifts at night so others could get a full night's sleep. I spent much of that night lying on the cold hard floor with a mock rifle in my hands in firing position. You'd be astounded how high a Drill Sergeant can leap when they open the bay door for a surprise inspection and find you staring at them down rifle sights. The squat thrusts I earned as punishment did nothing to aid my sleep.

Tuesday we began live fire exercises that allowed us to adjust the sights to our personal needs. We stood assured at the end of the day that should maniacal barns rise to threaten this great nation we would be able to hit their broadsides.

I didn't think it was funny either, but Drill Sergeant Smith said it all the same.

In the days that followed my time on the ceramic floor prepared me well. While others moaned and complained about spending hours on their elbows in sand and grass, it seemed a luxury to me. Sadly it did nothing to help my subpar performance at the firing range.

Kraft expounded at great length upon his theory that my preoccupation with bitches, while I blamed lack of experience firing a weapon of any kind before. Reality was between Monday and Friday morning I clocked a total of seventeen hours of sleep and I couldn't hold my hands steady no matter how hard I tried. When I saw a little girl in a white dress and hat skipping across the bay I got my first inkling that something was awry.

Saturday morning I went on a sick call. I intended to get something, anything, to help me sleep at night. I'd seen the little girl several times on Friday and I'd read somewhere that lack of sleep could make you see things. Wait, it wasn't something I read, it was an episode of Star Trek The Next Generation.

Instead of seeing a doctor I got referred to Community Mental Health Services. Hallucinations it turned out were their domain.

I spent the rest of the day sitting in a chair waiting in a room of twenty or so other soldiers, some in training like me, others with rank and unit patches. My first opportunity to interact with permanent party personnel as the Drill Sergeants called them.

"What phase are you in?" The man next to me asked, startling me.

"White phase," I said listlessly, then snapped my head around to check his rank. "Sergeant." I quickly added.

"Fun times, qualifying this week or next?" He asked.

"Wednesday," I replied.

"Let me give you a piece of advice. When it comes time to qualify ignore the two hundred and fifty and three hundred yard targets."

"Why would I do that Sergeant?"

"Simple math. You need to hit twenty-two out of forty targets. Nine of those are so far out only the talented few who pass through a company in any given cycle have any real chance of hitting them. Ignore them and you've got nine chances to squeeze off a second round at a closer target if you miss it with the first."

I did the math real quick, "Why not ignore the two hundred-meter targets too? That leaves twenty-three targets and seventeen extra rounds."

"You're right, but that only leaves a slim margin of error. You manage to miss two of those and you fail. With my method, you at least get a chance at placing sharpshooter instead of marksman too."

Given my performance over the last week, I needed every edge I could get.

A woman poked her head out the door and I turned hoping she'd call my name. When she didn't I turned back to resume my discussion with the sergeant, but he was gone. He hadn't left, I was facing the door. Then I noticed others watching, staring, waiting for me to continue conversing with an empty chair.

Those of us in training were ushered off to the cafeteria and back for lunch. Finally, before evening chow a woman came out and called my name. I stood and approached her and she handed me a slip of paper. "We weren't able to get you in to see a doctor today. You have an appointment at thirteen thirty on Monday." The bus brought me back to the battalion just in time to march my platoon off to the mess.

That night I got my first taste of pigs feet. Not what I was expecting, but certainly not bad, though I got the impression I was the only one in the company who dared give them a taste. After chow we, or at least the others, were released to pursue their wanton whims. Lt. Gates, however, would be expecting me at CQ.

"Enter," She said after an unusually long wait at her door.

Four steps in, snap, turn, snap, "Private Johnson reports as ordered ma'am."

"Good evening Johnson." She eyed me hungrily. "I understand you went on sick call today. What's wrong? Are we riding you too hard?" She ran a finger up my chest, liking her lips, and her finger stopped at my forehead. "And they sent you along to CMHS. What's going on in that head of yours Johnson?"

"Nothing a good night's sleep won't sure ma'am."

"You're not going to kill yourself are you Johnson?"

"Ma'am?"

"They usually only send privates off to CMHS if they are, or at least claim to be, suicidal." She raised an eyebrow. "Or homicidal."

"Nothing like that ma'am. Just trouble sleeping."

"If that's the case you may go up to your bunk and get some rest, or at least attempt to."

"I don't think that's necessary ma'am." Truth is I just didn't think it would work.

"Splendid." I remained at attention while she disappeared behind me. I heard the distinct sound of clothes hitting the floor. Her lips caressed my neck while her hands worked at my clothes. I yielded to her as she removed my clothes. She nibbled on my ear and her hand grasped my engorging cock. Her fingers gripped tightly, slowly working it until it was rock hard in her grasp, and I struggled to maintain my composure.

Suddenly, without the barest hinting, I was penetrated deep and hard, my bearing obliterated by the uncomfortable knee-weakening sensation. Both hands groped out of the edge of the desk lest I fall. I looked back over my shoulder relatively relieved to find Lt. Gates grinning back at me. "You like that Johnson?" She asked pulling out slowly, then ramming deep inside me once more.

A moan was my only answer, my legs wavering and my arms straining to hold myself aloft. My mind reeled from the pleasure I derived from her slow and purposeful thrusts. Time ceased to hold meaning, "harder" I uttered absently between gasping moans. Her fingers dug into my hips as she obliged. Again and again, the word ushered forth and I felt her straining behind me to thrust ever harder. "Oh god!" I screamed, my whole body convulsing in orgasm, my knees buckled and I collapsed to the floor.

Above me she stood, clad in a leather strap harness, a large veined dong hanging between her legs. She let the device fall around her ankles and perched herself on the edge of the desk and I watched as her fingers dipped between her thighs and groped at her breasts.

"That was fun, but it's completely unsatisfying for me." She said pouting at me between moans.

I lie there watching, waiting for the strength to return to my limbs, and oozing uncomfortably from my ass. She continued until the passions stirred in me once more, and I stood ready to give her what she desired. Like a wild primitive I knocked her backward and plunged into her dripping gash. Hoisting her legs up over my shoulders I thrust hard and deep determined to elicit screams from her as she had from me.

I don't recall it happening, but at some point, unsolicited and unintentionally I switched orifices, which Kraft would later term "pulling a dick nasty". She screamed and moaned, she shuddered and came, and so too did I, and when we were finished gasping greedily for air she glared at me, exhausted, and hissed the words, "Never again.

I withdrew and immediately resumed my rigid at-attention position. "Understood ma'am," I replied fearing the punishment that would come with my indiscretion.

Her head lulled back hanging over the edge of her desk, contemplating, I presumed, my punishment. Suddenly she popped up, sitting once more on the edge of the desk before me. "Christ I'm going to be sore tomorrow." She said pointing an accusing finger at me. "Proper lubrication next time Johnson."

"But you just said…" I replied full of confusion.

"At ease Johnson. I said never again were you to pull a switch up on me like that. Lord knows I love anal, but Christ you've got to use a ton of lube or you'll regret it the next day."

I relaxed considerably hearing those words and slumped over into the chair near at hand.

"If I had to guess I'd say you've never let anyone violate you like that before, am I right Johnson?"

"No ma'am, can't say I have."

"Sure did like it though didn't you?"

"I'd be lying if I said I didn't Lieutenant."

She lay back on her desk once more, limbs dangling. I saw by the clock the night already half passed. I heard her sigh, breasts heaving. "You are dismissed, Johnson."

I gathered up my clothing and walked to the door. My hand grasped the door knob and I paused for a moment. "Goodnight ma'am," I said.

"Goodnight Johnson." She replied, adding, "Get some sleep." as I pulled open the door. I donned my uniform in the hall and made my way up to my bunk, skipping out on the rest of the night's delights. I passed out without even bothering to pull back the blanket or take off my boots. I slept, as they say, like a baby.

6

Chapter 6

Sunday morning I awoke in someone's embrace. Drowsily I rolled over to find myself face to face with a blissfully sleeping Alicia. Confused but elated I pressed my lips to hers. Startled she awoke, flailing, and pushed me out of bed. Rubbing my head I sat up in time to see her fleeing out the bay doors.

Kraft stood over me, toothbrush hanging from his mouth. "What the hell was that?" He asked, offering me a hand.

"I'm not sure. I woke up, Alicia was spooning me, I kissed her, she woke up, tossed me from my bunk, and bolted."

"You are a scary sight in the morning." He replied.

"What time is it?" I replied, putting the matter aside.

"Oh-eight-thirty. Sorry to say you missed breakfast. You two looked cozy, so I didn't wake you."

"What time is mass again?" I said, opening my locker and grabbing a few sundries.

"I'm just about to leave. You coming along this time you heathen?"

"Yeah, give me five minutes." I rushed past him to the latrine to clean myself up and get looking presentable.

I packed myself into the pews next to Kraft and settled in for service. It became clear within the first few minutes of the Chaplain's sermon that the topic remained largely unchanged from the last time I'd attended. I soon drifted off into contemplation of Alicia who seemed to confound me at every turn. A band came out to play rock renditions of hymns and the whole chapel filled with song, to which I remained oblivious.

Between service and bible study I was accosted once more and thrust forcibly into the last stall of the female latrine.

"What the hell are you doing?" I blurted out before I even realized what was happening.

Alicia stood before me, eyes blazing fiercely, a finger hovering inches from my nose. "I'm setting you straight." She paused to let it sink in. "Last night I wandered downstairs looking to get away from the chaos. I saw someone lying asleep so I crawled into bed with them for comfort. I just wanted to hold on to someone. If I'd known it was you I cozied up to I would have sooner gone back up to the fuck fest and grabbed the first exhausted sweaty body available."

My heart sank.

"The sight of you makes me wretch. The mere thought of you... of you..." Tears began streaming from her eyes and she turned away sobbing.

"I love you." Unbidden the words leaped from my tongue.

"You son of a bitch." she said, punctuated by the sting of her hand across my face. "After all you've done..." She trailed off into a fit of sobbing. I reached out and dared to embrace her tightly in my arms. I heard someone enter the latrine and occupy the stall next to us. I prayed whoever it was would not take heed of the extra pair of boots visible beneath the stall walls.

Alicia sniffled and blew her nose into a hastily gathered fistful of toilet paper.

"Is everything alright?" The newcomer asked.

"I'm fine." Alicia managed to express without sounding distressed.

"You're sure?"

Alicia looked up into my eyes and nodded. "Yes, I'm fine." She replied. "Just fine."

I wiped the tears from her eyes with my thumbs and her head in my hands. She kissed me tenderly and the toilet in the other stall flushed. The sink ran, the automatic hand dryer blew, and the door closed, leaving us alone again.

"Do you mean it?" She asked once our lips parted.

I stared at her for a moment, pondering the very same question. "Of course I do," I replied, "Why would I lie?"

"What about Lt. Gates?"

"What about her?" A stupid question.

"Every week you go and see her and she has her way with you. She has her fill of you and I sit and I cry and you, well you do your duty without question." More tears.

"As long as she's our XO, there's not a whole lot I can do about that. If I defy her she can have me removed from the company, or worse yet the service entirely." Neither option was acceptable to me. She started sobbing again. "Listen, I'll do what I can to get out from under her, I promise I'll try, but that's all I can do."

"You promise?"

"I do." Her mood seemed suddenly to improve greatly. I looked at my watch. "We need to get out of here, it's almost time to get back on the bus to battalion." She kissed me and left to make sure the hall was clear so I could make my exit from the female Latrine without getting caught.

On the bus ride back we sat next to each other and held hands, though she was happily oblivious, I remained ever wary of catching the attention of someone else.

That night I lie sleeplessly in my bunk.

Monday morning we filed into the buses fully packed for bivouac. Weapon in hand I felt a shade of dread wash over me. Today, the first day of practice qualifications, promised to be a long day of failure.

After lunch I lie in the prone position, plugging in my ears, awaiting the signal for the second half of the qualifier to begin. Before lunch, my first round amounted to a resounding failure. Behind me, Drill Sergeant Greenway paced past. The horn sounded and Green silhouette targets popped up into place down range. Quickly I swept the barrel back and forth, squeezing the trigger as each caught my eye.

"What the hell are you doing Johnson?" I heard over my shoulder. "You didn't even fire at that fifty-yard target." In the corner of my eye, I saw the target in question pop back down and cursed as I missed the opportunity to fire at another. The alarm sounded, I flipped the weapon to safe and jammed a breech block into my rifle. I stood up to find Drill Sergeant Greenway glowering.

"How the hell do you not only miss but fail to even fire at a fifty-meter target? Are you blind or just stupid?"

"Blind it would seem, Drill Sergeant," I replied while the next group got into position on the range.

"You need to get your shit together soldier. Get the hell out of my face Johnson."

I spent the rest of the afternoon doing my best to lose myself in cleaning my rifle. The results of my second practice round won me the spot of second lowest in the platoon, and no amount of scraping carbon from the disassembled bolt, assembling and disassembling, and otherwise trying to focus on the weapon in my hands could spare my mind from dwelling on it. A hot meal and a long march to bivouac site D on the other hand did wonders to improve my spirits. At least until nightfall.

Sleeplessness is the bane of anyone out on a bivouac. Crammed inside a two-man tent, it's impossible to do anything beyond stare up into darkness. No room for flashlights and letter writing. No room to practice prone firing. No means to pick up extra fire guard patrolling. No privacy to jerk off. Maddening, lying there waiting for the first rays of sunrise to break through the tent flaps and single morning.

We tore down, packed up, and covered our tracks first thing upon waking. A cold prepackaged meal ranking somewhere below MREs in the opinion of most, we choked it down anyway, knowing all too well by this point not to turn down any food afforded us no matter how bad. Everyone got in formation and marched back out to the range, myself and three others excepted. The four of us remained behind to help the supply sergeant load trash and drink coolers onto the supply truck, then took it back to the battalion. The others went on sick call and I waited out the morning until lunchtime then went to my appointment at CMHS.

The waiting room held almost as many people as the last time I'd come. I scanned the room, to my relief the phantom sergeant from the weekend was not in attendance, and I took a seat.

An hour past my scheduled appointment a man called me back to his office, fourth door on the left. "Have a seat." He said closing the door behind us. "My name is Dr. DeMar and you are...?"

"Private Johnson sir," I replied.

"Right. Says here you haven't been sleeping. Tell me about that."

"Well sir, it's pretty straightforward. I haven't been able to get more than two or three hours of sleep a night in over a week."

"And how has that affected your training?" He asked, scribbling notes in my medical files.

"I've been unable to concentrate. I'm tired constantly. I can't remember anything I read. And I've been having hallucinations."

"What do you mean hallucinations?"

"Seeing things that aren't there. Can't be there." I answered.

"Can you give me an example?"

"A little girl in a white dress, I've seen her skipping around the bay or playing with the blinds. I saw a man I'd never seen before dressed in a gray suit walk into the latrine while I was cleaning it, enter a stall, and disappear when I went to confront him. Saturday when I was in your waiting room here I had an entire discussion with a Sergeant sitting next to me who wasn't there it turned out."

"What did you discuss?" He asked while scribbling further notes.

"Rifle qualification. He told me a trick to make it easier to qualify."

"Has that been something you've been concerned about the last week or so? Qualification?"

"A bit yeah. I didn't fare well on the ranges last week, and yesterday my practice qualifiers were abysmal."

"Did you try the trick your Phantom Sergeant imparted on you?"

I thought about it and realized that the entire incident had slipped my mind. "No sir I didn't."

"While I wouldn't normally suggest giving much credence to the things discussed with delusions, if it's something that will work, you may want to consider it. If you think about it, the idea came from your brain, perhaps as an attempt to relieve some of the stress and anxiety you've been feeling." He pulled a prescription pad out of his drawer and wrote something incomprehensible on it. "In the meantime, I'm going to prescribe you something that should help you sleep, and give you a waver to take your name off the fire guard roster for a few days." He handed me the script. "I want you to make an appointment to come back next week on your way out."

"Thank you, sir," I said, taking my leave. An hour and a half later I sat in CQ with a bottle of pills in my pocket and my nose buried in my training manual. Much to my annoyance the supply truck made its return trip to the range fifteen minutes earlier, leaving me to miss the opportunity for one last qualifier round before the big day tomorrow. My chances of qualifying seemed even less likely.

That night when I returned from chow the rest of the company returned, cheerfully abuzz about the perfect forty out of forty scored by the Russian kid in the third platoon. When I got a moment I congratulated him and wished him luck on a repeat performance the next day. If he managed it a second time it'd give real cause for celebration.

After a shower, I saw the little girl again skipping around the bay in her little white dress, wide-brimmed hat, and shoes. I walked to my locker and pulled out the pill bottle. I saw her stop and stare at me, as I shook two pills out into my palm. She coked her head to the side as if curious what I was doing. "Good-bye," I whispered and popped the pills into my mouth followed by a swig from my canteen. I climbed up into my bunk and within a few minutes passed out. I dreamed I had superpowers. Weird.

It took Kraft slapping me around to wake me the next morning, and I fell into formation in a haze barely aware of my surroundings. Someone asked me a question, and I answered, though I have no idea what either of us said. Breakfast helped slightly, but the bus ride to the range proved counterproductive as I nodded off and had to be practically shoved out of my seat to wake again. As impossible as it sounds I fell asleep again, rifle in hand, staring down the range and the targets. Needless to say, I failed to qualify first round. Sergeant Gunn made sure I was awake after lunch by making me run laps around the pavilion.

Second round I recalled what my phantom mentor impressed upon me, and invigorated by the PT, I shot a respectable twenty-eight and lifted a great weight from my shoulders. At the end of the day, five members of the company failed to qualify. Come morning they would be transferred to a different company in a different battalion starting the white phase on Monday.

Friday morning we received a pair of discipline cases from another company and as platoon Sergeant, it fell to me to get them squared away. They came from a battalion where they bunked six people to a room with S.O.P. so different nearly everything in our lockers was backward to them.

"I'm telling you, MP3 players are completely out of the question," I repeated for the third time. "If you get caught with those things you'll find yourselves back at golf company with a ticket home.

"You can't be serious." The taller of the two replied. "How do we know you aren't just fucking with us?"

"What would I gain from that?"

"Why wouldn't you?" The shorter one pushed aside a few things in his drawer to make room for a small stack of Maxim magazines.

"Jesus Christ, was there anything they didn't let you have in your old company?" I said grabbing the stack of magazines from his locker and tossing them back into his luggage.

"You mean we can't have magazines either? Man, we got transferred to hell." The two of them shook their heads with disdain.

"Do yourselves a favor and put that shit into your bags and forget it exists for the next four weeks."

Later, while we stood in formation after eating lunch, Drill Sergeant Greenway appeared up on the landing outside our bay. "You two dumb bastards spend two weeks at golf company and it takes you one day to fuck up." He yelled down to us, tossing the stack of Maxim magazines over the railing. "Johnson bring the two idiots who thought they could hide magazines from me up here now."

The three of us stood toeing the line that separated the center of the bay, the no men land off limits to all but the drill sergeants, behind us the two bunks of the newcomers lay tossed and torn apart.

"You two morons spent two weeks in Golf Company because of stupid shit like this and it takes you one day back in a real platoon to screw up."

"But he told us it was okay Drill Sergeant." The short little bastard replied. I wanted to punch the little bastard, but I remained at attention, staring straight ahead.

"Is that right Johnson? Did you set these two up for failure?"

"Not Drill Sergeant," I answered.

Greenway paced the floor for a moment. "Here's the problem. I've got you two boneheads claiming Johnson set you up. Johnson has been here for five weeks and has an exemplary record as a stand-up soldier. You on the other hand spent the last two weeks at Golf one-two-eight because well, I don't know what for, but you have to have done something stupid to end up there. That means your word isn't worth the stale breath that carried it to my ears against his." I suppressed a smile. "You two get to spend every night for the next week pulling a double shift of fire watch. Now get back downstairs the both of you." They made a quick retreat from the bay leaving me standing alone with a pissed-off instructor. "Johnson you're no longer platoon sergeant. Give me your stripes."

I removed the small pin from the flap of my left breast pocket and handed it to him.

"You fucked up Johnson. I expected you to get them straight up here. You're on CQ duty second shift Thursday nights until further notice."

"Understood Drill Sergeant."

"I'm giving your stripes to Garcia. Get back downstairs."

I marched my ass with precision out of the bay and fell into the third squad.

That night I took Garcia aside before lights out. "Listen, if you need help with anything you let me know."

"Don't worry I got things under control." He replied.

"You've had those stripes for all of five hours, don't think you understand everything that comes along with wearing them already."

He shook his head. "What's to understand? I march the platoon to chow, I assign people to fire guard shifts and other details. Most importantly I get to go stick it to Lt. Gates and you don't." He smiled.

While he may be the envy of every other man in the company, I gladly relinquished that last duty to him. "Suit yourself."

Saturday night Alicia's face lit up when I arrived with everyone else. To see her smiling like that softened the blow I suffered to my illustrious boot camp career. If nothing else the morons allowed me to deliver on my promise to get away from the clutches of our executive officer. We withdrew to her bunk and amid the roiling orgy around us made love sweet and tenderly in our little world. Afterward, we withdrew to the relative seclusion of her wall locker where we sat in each other's arms.

"How'd you get away?" She asked after our comfortable silence had worn thin.

"You remember when Drill Sergeant Greenway found the contraband the two new guys recycled from Golf Company yesterday?"

"No, I was on KP yesterday."

"Oh, well the two new guys decided they knew better than me when I told them to put a stack of Maxim magazines into their bags and decided to try to hide them. Drill Sergeant Greenway found the magazines while we were at lunch and I got stripped of my boot stripes because I failed to get them properly squared away."

"I'm sorry."

"No, you're not. You got exactly what you wanted."

She turned to look me in the eyes. "Is that so bad of me?"

"No not really." I remained bitter, but I knew I'd get over it. I reached into my pocket and pulled out my medication. I kissed her cheek and popped the pills into my mouth.

"Goodnight." She said, settling in with her head against my chest. I passed out there on the floor. In the morning Kraft informed me that he and a few others dragged my ass back to my bunk. Instead of going to church, I slept in the corner of my wall locker between meals.

7

Chapter 7

Beginning Monday we entered Blue phase, the final phase of basic combat training. We ceased to be selfish individuals and now it was time to bond and become a team. Imagine all the team-building exercises you've seen on sitcoms, or in movies, and you'll have a pretty good idea of what I'm talking about.

On Wednesday I missed out on team building for an appointment with Dr. DeMar. I voiced my complaints about the medicine making me sleep too much and he told me to take half the dosage in hopes that it would be enough to get me to sleep without leaving me lethargic in the morning.

Thursday night I reported walking down to CQ to relieve the females on duty. "Who's the NCOIC tonight?" I asked after formally relieving them of duty.

She shook her head. "No non-com tonight."

"The Captain?" I asked.

"Nope."

I sank into the chair behind the desk. As I feared Lt. Gates had a way to get at me even though I no longer made the Saturday evening reports. I pulled out my training manual and began repeating the nomenclature for various types of grenades. Perhaps an hour later she summoned me to her office.

"Private Johnson reports as ordered ma'am."

"Good evening Johnson." She smiled. "Got yourself into a bit of trouble I see. You shouldn't take it too hard though, I don't think any platoon sergeant has held onto his boot stripes through a whole cycle." She paused a moment to file away the stack of papers on her desk. "Can't say I care much for your replacement though."

"Ma'am?"

"He's like a little jackhammer, but without any stamina. All business. Don't get me wrong, he gets the job done, but it's over so fast. Very disappointing. I think I'll have him replaced."

"He'll be devastated," I replied.

"I'm sure."

She rose and kissed me hard. The verbal intercourse out of the way she got to the heart of what she desired. She thrust her tongue into my mouth and I yielded to her, we groped at each other's clothing. Once bare she toppled me over onto her desk and mounted me, shuddering and moaning instantly, as though just having me inside her was a pleasure of the most exquisite nature.

I lay there on the hard surface, held in the grasp of a petite woman's thighs grinding my ass against the Polish mahogany. My hands groped blindly at her body, her eyes opened long enough to betray the thrill derived from my touch. My mind drifted to Alicia. The devastation and betrayal she'd feel when she learned of this forbidden encounter. I felt orgasm wash over me, hollow, a release without pleasure. Like rubbing out a quick one when you're not really in the mood.

"What are you doing?" She stopped, one hand pushing hair out of her face and tucking it behind her ear. Perhaps the most feminine action I'd ever seen her take.

"What?" Confusion gripped me.

"What are you doing?"

"Umm... fornicating?"

You're stiff, tense, it's like fucking a corpse." She got up and pulled on her clothes. I didn't know how to respond and I didn't want to know how she'd come to that comparison. "What the hell is wrong with you Johnson?"

"I don't know ma'am. The medication maybe? I took it just before you called me in. I am rather drowsy." I lied.

"Perhaps." She donned the last of her uniform and returned to sitting behind her desk. "You are dismissed, Johnson. Next week refrain from taking your medication until after your shift. I can't have you drifting off on duty."

I spent the rest of my shift muttering nomenclature.

8

Chapter 8

The whole following day devoted to hand-to-hand combat left me sore, aching, and certain that shooting someone before they could get close enough to lay a hand on me suited me just fine. Saturday evening rolled around and I pulled Garcia aside for a moment before he set out.

"What do you mean watch my tailpipe?" He asked a little too loudly.

"Hey keep it down." I looked around to be sure no one else paid us mind. "I mean Lt. Gates has a strap on, and she likes to use it." He looked about to laugh hysterically, but I remained grimly serious. "If she goes for it all you can do is relax, stop clenching, and hope for the best." I patted him on the shoulder. "And remember. This stays between us."

When I went upstairs with everyone else for some much-needed R&R I found Alicia sitting on her bunk chatting with another girl seated on the bunk opposite to her. "Hi," I said taking a seat next to Alicia.

"Hi." The other girl, Dias, said. The two of them giggled.

"What's gotten into you?" I asked.

"Dias is my best friend, and we were talking," Alicia replied. "We both always wanted to have a threesome."

"I've never really thought about having a threesome." If Kraft heard me say that he'd declare me not a man.

"Well, we were thinking, what better place to explore this desire than this?" She was right, amid so many other people doing the same, what better context existed?

"Why not," I replied.

All the permission they needed lay in that vague answer and they immediately set about stripping me from the waist down. They took turns licking and stroking my engorging cock

"Big and thick just like you said," Dias said to Alicia before slowly taking it all into her mouth. The deeper it went the more certain I became she would gag on it any moment. To my surprise, she made it down before letting it slip back out over her tongue and back in. Meanwhile, Alicia hurried about undressing herself, and I staring into Dias's eyes, removed my remaining clothing.

Alicia took me in her hand and pumped vigorously while Dias stripped off her uniform. I grasped the underside of the bunk to steady myself, moaning softly. Dias kissed her hard and their tongues entwined, while her fingers thrust deep between Alicia's thighs. Alicia responded in kind with her free hand.

Alicia took a turn sword swallowing, and Dias slide up next to me on the bed kissing me passionately while I toyed with her clit. I played torturously with her desires in between my gasps and moans. Wordlessly they left me to watch and moved to eat each other, stacked together like pornographic Lego bricks. I moved to one end and started plugging away at Alicia, but soon found Dias' head banging against my stomach too awkward. I tried instead moving around to the other side where I slid into Dias's surprisingly tight pussy, which proved far less awkward.

I pounded Dias hard and fast, the bunk lurching beneath us, rattling with the force I exerted upon her. Her head leaned back and she begged for more. I threw every ounce of leverage I could into plowing her. Finally, I blew my load deep inside her, then pulled out and sat back exhausted. I watched them continue pleasuring each other, Dias dripping and oozing all over Alicia's face. I chuckled slightly having indirectly blown a load on Alicia's face.

Once they satisfied each other Dias kissed me and wobbled off toward the latrine. Alicia, face drenched and eyes clenched shut groped about blindly. I took her hand and said in her ear, "Let's go get you cleaned up." I led her through the tangled knots of people into the showers. I pushed all the viscous fluids from her eyes and kissed her gently. Borrowing someone else's soap we washed each other in silence. Clean and dry we retired to her bunk. No sign of Dias.

"Was she better than me?" Alicia said from her place nested against my chest.

"What? No, what are you talking about." I answered defensively.

"You sure sounded like you were having a good time."

"Wasn't that the point?"

"You don't moan like that when you're fucking me." She sat up, arms folded, eyes seething.

"You enjoyed fucking her more than you do me. Admit it, she's better than me."

"You're imagining things. Besides it was your idea in the first place."

"That didn't stop you from agreeing to it. Am I that horrible that you were glad to bring someone else in to liven things up?"

"It was your idea."

"They why did you pull out of me and go fuck her instead?"

"Jesus, is that what this is about? I only did that because it was too awkward the other way. Christ Alicia, it was nothing more than logistics."

"Bullshit." She flung herself down and buried her face in a pillow.

I did the only thing I could, I held her. "I love you," I whispered. We fell asleep with nothing resolved. I skipped church the next morning.

"No quality time with the Lord today Johnson?" Kraft asked dropping his laundry bag and slumping down next to me.

"The Lord will get over it," I said over the sound of washers and dryers.

"I saw you putting it to Dias last night. The girl is a freak."

"Why? Wouldn't give it up to you?" I smiled.

"Oh she gave it up, they all do eventually. No, she's a freak because she wanted me to choke her while we were doing the deed." He wrapped his hands around an imaginary neck to illustrate.

"You didn't."

"Hell yeah, I did. Doesn't change my opinion of her though."

"You, my friend, are a freak."

"You don't even know." Kraft jumped the line and claimed an open washing machine. "I've nailed damn near every piece in this company and most of them have one kink or another. Shit Johnson, you think choking is bad, Owens is a damn furry."

"Dare I ask what a furry is?" I suspected I didn't want to know.

"Never heard of furries? Furries are goofy bastards that get off on dressing like animals, and I'm talking about full-blown amusement park mascot, animals when they get it on. Now that's some freaky shit. I've even heard of some getting cat whisker implants."

I was right, I could have lived without that knowledge. "Freaky."

"Seeing as it's you down here I'm going to go clean the sand out of my locker."

"No problem," I replied.

He left while I pulled someone's dry clothes out of a dryer and put them into the laundry back, switched someone else's load over into the dryer, and put the next-in-line bag of clothes into the washer. When I finished I found myself not entirely alone.

"I don't like your friend." The little girl in white stood before me.

I took a seat, putting myself roughly at her eye level. "Why not?"

"He's perverse. It's unpleasant the way he speaks of women." She replied from underneath her wide-brimmed hat.

"You're not wrong." I realized then that I'd forgotten my medication the night before.

"I don't know why you like him so much."

"He's a good guy. A walking stereotype, but a good guy nonetheless." I pondered the significance of the conversation at hand. "Who are you anyway? What do you want.?"

"I want to be your friend. You're nice, but you take those awful pills that make me go away."

"I have to sleep. You can't fault me for that." I replied feeling defensive.

"I guess not."

"I'm sure you're a great kid and all, but that's just the way it has to be."

"I guess so. I'm going to go play. See you later." She spun on her heels and disappeared out the door.

I made a note in the back of my manual to ask the doctor whether or not it was healthy to indulge in delusions and engage them in conversation.

In week seven we devoted all our time to training with what I like to call "the fun stuff." Grenades, under barrel grenade launchers, squad automatic weapons, claymore mines, and anti-tank rocket launchers. Much of this training meant handling dummy weapons. Grenades with no charge inside, previously fired launchers, and fake mines, but at least we got to toss a few real grenades and pour fifty rounds through a machine gun.

Thursday night I sat at the CQ desk waiting for Lt. Gates to call me into her office. In my hand I held the pill bottle, weighing whether or not I should pop the pills now and hope they knocked me out before she summoned me. Ultimately I thought better of risking the woman's ire.

Much like last week she pinned me down on top of her desk. I lie there, hands trailing lightly over her skin, while she rode me. Her moans escalated to screams and pleas to god before she curled up atop me, her pussy quivering from aftershocks. She stayed there, cuddled up to my chest so long I thought she'd fallen asleep. Not wanting to disturb her I lay on the hardwood desk waiting for my shift to come to a close. Eventually, she got up, cleaned herself up, and sent me out of her office in time to be formally relieved by the soldiers on the next shift.

Have you ever tried to have a long-distance relationship, perhaps Internet-based? Trying to have a relationship with a fellow soldier in basic training is much the same, with one notable difference. You see each other constantly. Up close, throughout the day, but just out of reach. If you think sitting around all day waiting for the love of your life to pop online and reply to your e-mail, or sign into your messenger flavor of choice is unbearable, you know nothing of torment. These are the things that occupied my thoughts throughout Saturday morning while I made sure every last thing in my wall locker was precisely in place.

That night I greeted Alicia with a firm embrace. When I tried to kiss her she turned away and withdrew to the relative privacy afforded by the doors of her wall locker.

"Wouldn't you rather kiss Dias?" She asked coldly when I approached.

"Would you forget about that? Please? What do Indeed to say to convince you I don't give a fuck about her?" I retorted, trying to enfold her in my arms again.

"You sure liked her last week." She broke away from my grasp.

I leaned back, banging my head on the locker behind us. "You don't see me getting all bent out of shape about you moaning while she was tongue fucking you."

"Don't you dare try to make this about me?" She screamed.

"Christ would you keep it down." I moved closer to her. "This is about you. It's your damn insecurity, your paranoia. You brought Dias into this and now you're all bent out of shape over some imagined connection between me and her. I'm here with you. I'm not looking for Dias hoping to get her to come join us again. I'm not downstairs with Lt. Gates. Doesn't that prove anything to you?" I reached out and grabbed her hand before she could draw it away. "Think about it. I'll be over there on the bunk when you figure out what you want."

She stood there trembling, fragile. Her uniform looked out of place like she were a child who snuck in to play make-believe. I sat on the edge of the bed staring at the floor. Did I look like her? A child playing warrior. Maybe that's all any of us were. People playing games never believing we'd ever go to war, get shot at, or kill anyone. All a game.

"What are you thinking about?"

"How beautiful you are even all trussed up as a killing machine." I lied. The last thing either of us needed was a philosophical debate at the moment. She took the bait and smiled. "You know no one else in this blasted company means anything to me." I paused for a moment then added. "Except maybe Kraft. I mean when you live that close to a guy for this long certain bonds start to form."

"Stop, stop, I don't want to hear about your male bonding." She hugged me, and I held her tight. She looked up at me, smiling broadly. "Tell me more about me."

I knew then that the whole Dias matter came to an end. I combed through my mind for the right words to say. Words she would never forget.

Your eyes are like pools shimmering deep
   Gods should will they never weep
   In the tragedy is the greatest sin
   when pain in ripples echo within
   What perfection exists to behold
   There is no other when all is told

Those words, stolen as they were from a writer named Drake Harlem, and I held her enraptured.

"Tell me you love me."

"I love you," I replied.

We spent the rest of the night talking. Something I'll admit we should have done sooner. I learned all about her mother, at home battling cancer, her oafish overbearing father, and most importantly her first boyfriend. Johnny spent most of the time they were together comparing her to other girls, ones he'd fucked, and others he wanted to. Her broke up with her every week only to come back claiming it was all a joke, he was in a bad mood, or whatever other excuse he could sucker her back to his side with. In the end, he fucked her best friend and she never spoke to either of them again.

I understood then why she reacted the way she did, not just to Dias but to Lt. Gates. If we'd gotten to know each other better in the beginning I never would have agreed to a three-way with her and anyone else. Her reaction, in the face of her past, made perfect sense.

9

Chapter 9

The next morning I found myself skipping church to hang out in the laundry room once more with Kraft sitting opposite me against a washer. "You realize, in two weeks, we'll be gone right?" I asked over top of my manual.

"Hell yeah, we will." He replied

"No more group showers, no more sharing a room with sixty other guys."

"No more orgies," Kraft added.

"No more orgies." I echo.

"Did I tell you I'm getting back with my old lady?"

"What? Since when?"

"We've been writing to each other since week one. I never realized how much I missed her until we spent so much time apart. I told her in my last letter, and she wrote back she felt the same."

"And yet the orgies."

"I said I was getting back with her, not that I was back with her."

"You are a man of complex morals my friend." I shook my head. "What she doesn't know won't hurt her I suppose."

"Screw that noise she knows all about the orgies. She also knows this is a very stressful place, and what better way to relieve that stress than getting your rocks off."

"All women should be so enlightened."

"Damn right, they should."

"Well damn man, congratulations. I hope it works out for you."

"You and me both brother."

Monday began with an early rise, called to formation, and filed into one of the classrooms. Bleary eyed we sat and waited for the other two companies to file in behind us. Finally, the room packed to capacity, Lt. Colon Buckley entered the room and addressed us. "Good morning. For those of you who don't know me, I'm Battalion commander Lt. Colonel Buckley. We are gathered here because hostile raiders have been harassing villages to the north and you are being deployed nearby to repel their attacks. At 14:00hrs. Each company will march ten miles to their assigned sights and set up for prolonged engagement."

By 17:00hrs Alpha company established a perimeter of fighting positions, better known as fox holes, at field exercise site E. Shortly thereafter Kraft and I enjoyed a meal of MRE inside our hole.

Over the week we engaged in mock battles, cycling tons of blank cartridges through our rifles directed at the few selected from our company to play the part of OpFor, while they did the same. We went on patrols, rescued dummies from behind enemy lines, and got gassed without warning time and again. As much fun as it sounds, in reality, the events got stale after the first two days.

Thursday night, after exchanging fire with OpFor for the second time that day, Kraft and I received permission to retire for the night to our two-man shelter.

"You're going to be cuddling up to your rifle alone tonight Johnson. I've got a date with a pair of foxes and their holes." Kraft said as he hoisted himself up out of our entrenchment.

"What with whom?"

"Two or three girls from the third platoon. Your friend Dias among them."

"Be sure to choke her extra hard for me," I said jokingly.

"Will do."

As soon as night fell he set out on his adventure. Sometime later, while I slept, I received a visitor of my own. I awoke with lips nibbling on my neck and a hand vigorously rubbing my crotch.

"Hey, baby," I uttered drowsily.

"Excuse me private?" Lt. Gates replied curtly, hands and lips called to a halt.

"Sorry ma'am you caught me off guard." I apologized.

"Weren't expecting someone else were you?"

"No Ma'am."

"Good, now get out of those sweaty clothes and come outside. It's nearly impossible to have sex inside one of these little tents."

Outside I found her bathed in moonlight. Her hair hung long and loose falling over her shoulders and concealing her breasts. A pale goddess of the night stood in place of the hard-polished soldier.

"I took the liberty of arranging some privacy for us. You don't mind do you?" Her fingers traced playfully up and down my chest. Somewhere distant I heard moans and screams. Kraft working on his craft.

Slip betwixt is beast, not man

Primal, driven with a singular purpose

on virgin blood it longs to feast

to spread its seed where it finds purchase

I whispered the words and took her in my arms.

"So you're a poet now are you?" She asked lips nibbling once more on my neck.

"No ma'am. Just quoting an author, one of my favorites." I replied gazing up at the fullness of the moon.

"Classical?" She inquired.

"Science fiction. Modern."

"Interesting."

"You like science fiction ma'am?"

"Occasionally. I wouldn't go far enough to say I'm a big fan."

"What you mean to say is you're not a nerd am I correct ma'am?"

"Precisely."

We stood there under the thin canopy of trees pierced here and there by moonbeams, stark naked. I felt something magical there, a liberation from station and rank, we stood there as equals, as peers.

She took my hand and we lay together pressed against each other in the cool grass. We kissed and all breath left me. The world dropped away and we were borne on the wind. For eons we wafted and deep inside me something stirred, without shape or definition, but unfettered now for the first time. My heart raced.

Our lips parted and we bound to earth again. Our eyes opened and fixed on each other. Something in her changed as well. She softened and became a delicate thing to be guarded closely. She felt the change too, her eyes shone with it.

I too her there in the grass on her hands and knees like wild things and for the first time she yielded to me completely. The control lies in my hands. I worked in her again and again, slowly and tenderly, while her moans echoed out into the night. We climaxed together, so in synch were we, and we curled up together under the stars. On the cusp of sleep, we held each other, breathing in time, and utterly at peace.

Gunfire broke the silence of the night and we scrambled for the tent where I grabbed my rifle and scrambled into the hole scanning the night for someone to fire at. The exchange of fire grew more and more distant as the fun-loving folks of OpFor took their raid to other parts of the encampment, then inevitably subsided. Behind me, someone came tromping heaving through the brush.

"Identify yourself," I said as quietly as possible.

"Sleigh bells."

"Bobsled." I gave the countersign and lowered my weapon.

"It's me, Alicia." She said stepping into the light.

I hung in the shadows, realizing the horrible situation I found myself in. "What are you doing here? I asked from the hole.

"The OpFor raid woke me up so I decided to come over here and see if you were awake."

Lt. Gates chose that moment to reveal herself from the tent, standing fully in the moonlight, stark naked with a couple of twigs in her hair. My ill-conceived plans unmade, I pulled myself out of the hole and revealed myself in the light.

Alicia looked as though she would explode at any moment. Silently she raised her rifle and unloaded an entire magazine worth of blanks at me. I stood there phased by the malice inherent in the ultimately harmless act. She stalked off, tears rolling down her cheeks.

"Who was that?" Lt. Gates asked standing beside me.

"Private Riordan ma'am."

"The two of you had a relationship I take it."

"As much as two people can have a relationship one night a week."

"I see now why you chose not to spend your nights with me."

"Yes ma'am she was."

"Girl like that is trouble, Johnson. I'd bet my commission that when family day rolls around her boyfriend comes to visit from back home and she pretends the last eight weeks never happened."

"She loves him very much."

"What's that?"

"She and I met on the bus ride from the airport. She told me all about her boyfriend back home."

"It's for the best then." She looked up at the sky.

"What about you ma'am?"

"I don't know Johnson. Eight weeks ago you were a plaything to be enjoyed for nine weeks, like many before."

"I'll be gone in a week."

"I know, but I'm not sure how I feel about that."

"Permission to get dressed ma'am. It's starting to get cold out here."

"Granted. I need to get back to CQ anyway. Lt. Col. Buckley will be there before much longer and I need to look presentable when he arrives."

I pulled my clothes out of the tent and donned them, while she did the same. A bitter chill on the wind served as a harbinger of a wet and miserable day. She stood before me and kissed me lightly, robbing me of my breath, then turned to leave.

"Ma'am," I said reaching out to her. She turned around and I brushed a twig from her hair.

"Thank you." She said.

After she left I lay down in the grass and watched the sunrise. Silently Kraft approached and stood over me.

"Sleighbell," I said, staring up at him.

"Bobsled." He replied with the countersign. "I understand we have our illustrious XO to thank for last night's booty call." He said with a smile.

"Yup," I answered.

"Why do you look so glum about it then?" He asked sitting down next to me.

"Alicia showed up."

"While you were doing the deed?"

"After."

"What did she say?"

"Nothing."

"Nothing? Nothing at all?"

"She shot me, well shot at me. At least half a mag unloaded straight at my head."

"Bitches."

"Nothing but tricks and hoes."

"Listen forget about all that bullshit. Those OpFor sons of bitches stole our platoon banner during that raid last night. Garcia got permission from Drill Sergeant Gunn to take a few of us and go reclaim it. Or better yet to steal Drill Sergeant Greenway's OpFor flag."

I sat up and grabbed my rifle. "Let's do this shit."

We grabbed Garcia and Rascon and the four of us set out on our mission.

10

Chapter 10

Midday passed and my stomach growled loud enough for Kraft to hear it ten feet to my left. For over an hour, the four of us lie spread out concealed by the bushes about 50 yards from the OpFor perimeter. OpFor currently sat in their fighting positions eating lunch. In the center of their small encampment, we saw our platoon banner flicking in the breeze, with a giant Airborne flag waving above it.

DS Greenway appeared from behind his tent and stood between the two fighting positions nearest to us. "You four come with me, we're providing enemy fire for a rescue mission."

"That dummy of theirs just won't stay out of trouble will he Drill Sergeant?" One of the soldiers asked as they hauled themselves out of their fighting positions.

"No soldier he won't. Now let's go see if we can put the fear of god into your fellow soldiers." He replied leading them off in the general direction of where Kraft and our squad had rescued the very same dummy just yesterday.

As soon as he was gone the rest of OpFor gathered together to talk. After some argument, they decided no one was going to bother their encampment and thus needed to leave no one behind while they went out to stir up trouble. Weighed down with smoke and gas grenades they vanished into the forest to our left.

Giving the others a signal to move me, we crawled along as far as we could before hitting open ground. From there we dashed the remaining distance, leaping across the tops of the fighting positions to where the flags lie. Quietly we lowered the airborne flag from its pole and then carefully folded it up.

"Let's move," Garcia said, ready to bolt from the scene.

"Wait," I said. "I've got a better idea." I held up a pair of gas grenades.

As quickly as possible we rigged up smoke and gas traps on everything we could think of. Even if none of them ever went off, OpFor would spend the better part of the evening disabling them all.

Banner and flag in hand we trudged through the forest by our circuitous route to avoid coming across OpFor on the way back. We returned triumphant in the early evening to accolades and cheers from those who saw us march up to CQ and return our banner to its place before presenting Drill Sergeant Gunn with the airborne flag. So swept up in the praise were we that we forgot about our aching empty stomachs. The prestige we found well worth the price of a few missed meals.

That night I slept soundly and for the first time woke up rested and refreshed in the morning. Saturday our mission was declared a success and we devoted the entire day to tearing down tents, filling in fighting positions, and otherwise making it appear as though we were never there. By the time we finished dinner was upon us and we ate the first hot meal in a week. After which we all gathered together in a clearing, kicked back against our packs, and relaxed. The drill sergeants themselves seemed more at ease, friendly, and cracking jokes with the rest of us. We took a short nap because there would be no wild hedonism that night. Instead, we had a fifteen-mile long haul back to the battalion, packs on our backs, through the darkness of night.

At Oh-Six-Hundred we crested the final hill and battalion came into full sight. Eager to slough off our gear and hit the rack we came upon a graduation ceremony of sorts waiting for us. We stood exhausted but honored as Lt. Col. Buckley delivered his speech and then our Drill Sergeants shook our hands and congratulated us. As of that moment, holding Drill Sergeant Gunn's hand I realized we were no longer students learning to crawl and walk on our own like children, but equals, brothers.

We retired to our bays perhaps an hour later, too tired to strip off our dirty sweaty uniforms, most of us immediately crashed on our bunks. No morning reveille awoke us, and we were allowed to sleep in well past lunch. A rest well earned and much needed.

Last week we did little more than thoroughly clean all of our gear and turn it in for the next cycle to use. Each day our lockers got emptier and emptier. The atmosphere around the company area completely changed and we had a freedom not known to us in the last nine weeks. ON family day that freedom extended even further, allowing those with visitors to wander the entire base. Though I had no visitors Lt. Gates permitted me to spend the day with Kraft, his ex, and their son.

I saw Alicia while we were out, clinging tightly to the arm of a young man who appeared somehow smaller than she. If she so much as looked my way I never saw it. Like everyone else, she pretended all the wanton reckless sex never occurred. Maybe it would never come to light for those with loved ones, but it mattered little to me. I arrived with no one and I left with no one.

Friday and Saturday we said our goodbyes as everyone trickled out to their next assignments by bus and by plane. I never saw most of them again, but I remember their faces and many of the names that go with them.

Kraft and several others accompanied me to AIT to receive the same training. Just as we gathered our things to catch the bus out of town Lt. Gates approached me and handed me a letter. She bade us farewell and we left the battalion behind.

Thanks For Reading

Now that you've finished reading I would greatly appreciate it if you spared me another minute to review the book. Just click on this big beautiful link and fire away with your irrational hatred or undying love. Also acceptable is anything in between those two extremes. Reviews really do help me out quite a bit and I take the time to read them as they come in so I can continue to improve and evolve as a writer.

Want some more dirty hot action? Click Here or Scan the QR code below to check out the rest of the Earth's Sexiest Heroes series.

Want to get in touch? Send me an e-mail: tom@richtererotica.com

About the Author

Tom Richter is a man with entirely too much free time on his hands and a brain full of boundless amounts of smut. Master of turning just about anything into some sort of innuendo or inspiration for his next literary romp, he is, without a doubt, a national treasure and a boon to the horny and unfulfilled the world over. Also he's ~~quite charming and totally single if you're interested~~ kind of a dick.

More than a little mad, but not a bit angry, Tom Richter spends his days feeding one hundred monkeys, who bang away at one hundred keyboards, occasionally regurgitating a book or two for him to send out in the world to earn more money for monkey food. It's a perpetual cycle, but it's fulfilling in a way that only a house full of monkeys can be. It may sound like some manner of monkey sweatshop, but it's really a nice, loving community of primates and the moron who decided to cram one hundred monkeys into his apartment to bang out books of erotic fiction. Tom also enjoys pickles.

www.ingramcontent.com/pod-product-compliance
Lightning Source LLC
Chambersburg PA
CBHW071633140626
46555CB00022B/2765